Gothic GRANGE
and the
Ghoul's Gold

Gothic GRANGE
and the Ghoul's Gold

Timothy Knapman

Maxine Lee-Mackie

Collins

Contents

School trip letter 2
Chapter 1 The school trip 4
Gothic Grange map 14
Chapter 2 The house 16
Real secret passages 26
Chapter 3 The quest 28
Real secret rooms...................... 36
Chapter 4 The ghost................... 38
Chapter 5 The horse................... 48
Real lost treasure 56
Chapter 6 The treasure................. 58
The secrets of Gothic Grange 68
About the author 70
About the illustrator.................... 72
Book chat.............................. 74

School trip letter

Tudor Manor School
Little-Riddle-on-the-Solve
Clewisham

Dear Parent or Guardian,

This term's school trip is to Gothic Grange, home of the famous Victorian author, Guy Languish.

Not suitable for children who are allergic to: old buildings, knights or ghosts.

Yours sincerely,

Mrs Rhodes

Itinerary:

9:00 a.m.	Depart from the school
10:00 a.m.	Arrive at Gothic Grange
10:00 a.m.	Welcome by Ms Mary Spector, the guide
10:30 a.m.	Tour of the house
12:30 p.m.	Lunch
1:00 p.m.	Free time, children can explore the gardens (risk assessment attached)
2:00 p.m.	Reading of Guy Languish's book *Sir Kay and the Adventure of the Riders of the Lost Bark*
3:00 p.m.	Depart
4:00 p.m.	Arrive back at the school

Chapter 1
The school trip

It was the day of the school trip and Liam Newitt was first to get on the coach. While he was waiting for everyone else, Liam read his book. It was called *Sir Kay and the Adventure of the Ghoul's Gold*. It was the most exciting book he'd ever read.

Sir Kay was the bravest knight in the land. Many months before, he had set out from Castle Valiant in search of treasure.

It was not just any treasure, but the legendary lost loot of Sir Grotesque Ghoul, the Ghost Knight. Sir Kay had already escaped from the Dragon's Maze, survived the Spinning Fire and flown on the back of Pegasus. Only one more challenge awaited him before he could claim the Ghoul's Gold. It would mean risking his life, but Sir Kay wasn't afraid. He was a knight of honour. He would be brave and complete his quest.

"The time has come," said Sir Kay, "to face the greatest danger of all."

Liam was about to turn the page and find out how the story ended when he felt a tap on his shoulder. It was his teacher, Mrs Rhodes.

"I've got a friend to sit next to you," she said.

Liam looked up to see who she meant. *Oh no*, he thought.

Coming down the middle of the coach towards him, with her bag dragging on the floor and her cardigan buttoned all wrong, was Suzy Upshot!

Suzy always made Liam worry. Liam was neat, polite and well-behaved. Suzy was messy, noisy and always getting into trouble. He never knew what she was going to do next and he worried that she'd get him into trouble too.

7

"But – " Liam started. He looked quickly around the coach, hoping he'd see another empty place. But, while he was reading, the coach had filled up with other children and there was nowhere else for Suzy to sit.

"Thank you, Liam," said Mrs Rhodes. Before he could stop her, she was walking back to her seat.

Suzy didn't say "Hello" or "Excuse me", she just climbed over Liam so that she could sit by the window.

"Careful!" Liam said. He had to hold his book up high so that she wouldn't mess up the pages. She still managed to tread on him and get muddy footprints all over his trousers and coat!

"Ouch!" said Liam, brushing the mud off.

He hoped that, once Suzy was comfortable, she'd leave him alone. No such luck! She started humming this annoying tune that seemed to go on forever. Worst of all, it stopped him concentrating on his book. He was going to say something when Suzy elbowed him in the ribs.

"What are you reading?" she asked.

Liam wanted to say "Nothing — because you aren't letting me!" but that would just make Suzy worse, and he wanted to be left alone. Instead, he said, "It's called *Sir Kay and the Adventure of the Ghoul's Gold*. It's about this knight and he's going on a thing called a 'quest'. That's a special adventure where you have to find something, a bit like a treasure hunt, but there are all these dangers along the way."

"Sounds really boring," said Suzy.

"It's not!" Liam insisted. "It's by a writer from the time of Queen Victoria called Guy Languish. We're going to visit his house today. I thought I should read one of his stories before we got there."

Suzy started making loud, rhythmic snoring noises. Liam didn't care. He would just get back to his book. With a bit of luck, he'd finish the story in time.

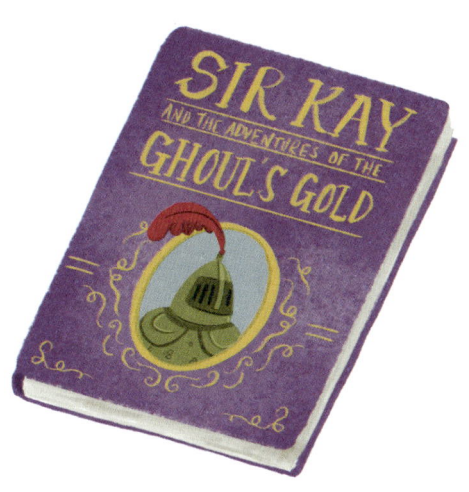

But soon, Suzy started humming her tune again. It was exhausting! After staring at one of the pictures for over a minute, Liam put the book away.

"Told you it was boring," said Suzy.

Liam took comfort from the thought that, once they were off the coach, he wouldn't have to see Suzy again all day.

Then Mrs Rhodes got up and announced, "This is a very big house we're visiting, with lots of rooms. I don't want anyone getting lost. I want you to pair up with the person sitting next to you. You must stay in that pair for the rest of the day."

"Great," Liam sighed. "That's the whole trip ruined."

Gothic Grange map

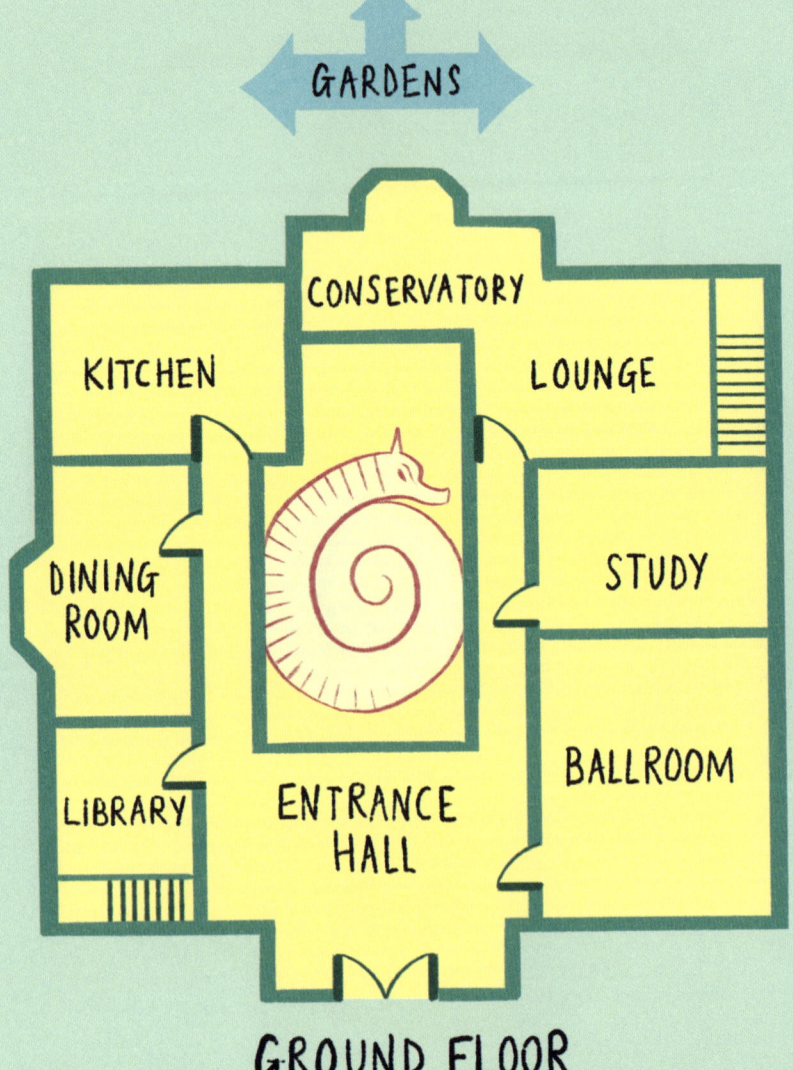

GROUND FLOOR

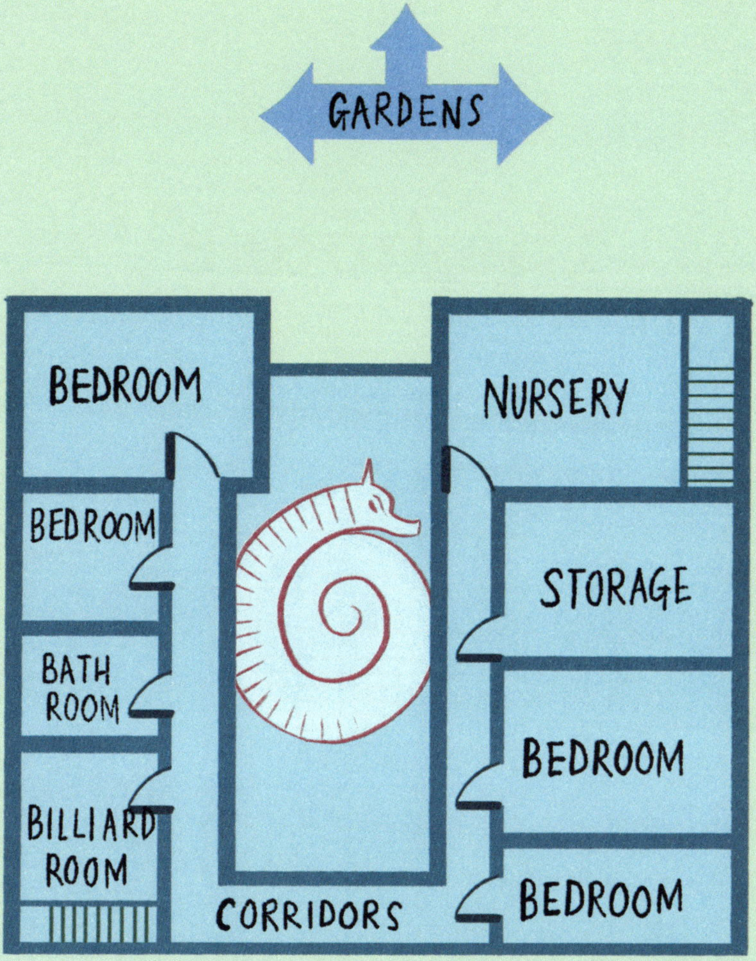
GARDENS
BEDROOM
NURSERY
BEDROOM
STORAGE
BATH ROOM
BEDROOM
BILLIARD ROOM
CORRIDORS
BEDROOM

FIRST FLOOR

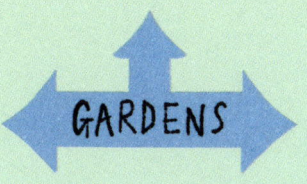

Chapter 2
The house

Mrs Rhodes had been right about one thing. Gothic Grange, the house they were visiting, was seriously big. The exterior looked like a church crossed with a castle. Monstrous gargoyles perched on its walls. Its roof was cluttered with towers and battlements.

"Wow!" said Liam.

Suzy yawned. Liam ignored her. He'd love to live in a house like this. No wonder Guy Languish wrote such brilliant books here.

The massive front door creaked open. Liam was almost expecting a knight to come galloping out on a horse. Instead, they saw a woman in trainers, jeans and a T-shirt. "Welcome to Gothic Grange, kids!" said the woman with a smile. "My name's Mary, I look after the place. I guess it seems a bit boring, right?"

Liam couldn't believe his ears. Suzy laughed out loud.

"But there's a rumour that this place is … haunted," Mary went on.

Some of the other children started chattering excitedly. Mrs Rhodes told them to be quiet and listen.

"This house belonged to Guy Languish, a boring — sorry, a *distinguished* old writer," said Mary, "but people say he hid some treasure here. He called it 'the Ghoul's Gold' and people say it's guarded by an actual ghost. No one's ever found the treasure, but some have seen the ghost! So, keep your eyes peeled when you go inside — just in case. Before we do that, I'd like to give you a guided tour of the gardens. Come with me."

The gardens turned out to be just as interesting as the house. They were dotted with gushing fountains, solemn temples and intriguing caves. There was even a waterfall that came thundering down a ravine. Liam thought it was like stepping into the story he'd been reading!

"Now let's go inside," smiled Mary, "and see if you can find any of that spooky treasure."

Mary led them into a large entrance hall with tall columns. It was filled with antique statues of knights and pictures of dragons. "I have a few chores to do," said Mary, "so I'm going to leave you and your teacher to have a look around. Some of the rooms are locked, I'm afraid, but there's still plenty to explore. Have fun – and keep an eye out for that ghost!"

The other children clapped as Mary walked off. Liam didn't want to be rude, but he didn't like the way Mary had called Guy Languish boring.

"Everybody stay in your pairs and follow me," said Mrs Rhodes.

Liam looked around for Suzy but she was nowhere to be seen. He guessed she'd wandered off. Honestly! He wasn't going to let Suzy get him into trouble. He'd just have to find her before Mrs Rhodes noticed they were missing.

Suzy hadn't gone far. She was walking along one of the corridors off the entrance hall, trying all the doors to see if any of them were unlocked.

"What are you doing?" said Liam urgently. "They're going on without us."

"So what?" Suzy shrugged. "I want to find this treasure."

"It's just a silly story," said Liam. At that moment, the door handle Suzy was trying clicked and the door opened.

"We'll see," she said, smiling slyly, and she disappeared into the room.

"Come back!" said Liam, running in after her.

There was a big desk in the room and the walls were lined with bookcases. It must have been Guy Languish's study — the room where he wrote all his books! Liam couldn't help getting excited. He pulled back the chair and sat at the desk.

"What's the name of that book you were reading on the coach?" asked Suzy. She was over by one of the bookcases.

"*Sir Kay and the Adventure of the Ghoul's Gold*," Liam replied without thinking. Then he wondered why Suzy would want to know.

"Found it," Suzy said. "Catch!" She was going to pull the book off the shelf and throw it at him. The book would be ruined!

"Don't — be careful!" Liam cried.

23

But the book wouldn't come off the shelf. Instead, it tilted like a lever.

There was a rumbling noise and the bookcase swung slowly open with a loud creak. Beyond it, a shadowy corridor stretched off into the darkness.

"Oh, wow, a secret passage!" said Suzy.
"Well, that's a start…"

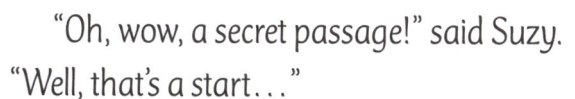

Real secret passages

Gothic Grange isn't the only building to contain a secret passage. There are plenty around the world that you can visit. Here are some …

Bran Castle in Romania has a secret staircase. It's hidden behind a fireplace. In the past it allowed people to escape to a higher part of the castle when it was under attack.

Bran Castle

the secret staircase

This palace in France is where the French king and queen lived. When they wanted peace and quiet, they disappeared into secret rooms.

Chapter 3
The quest

"Where are you going?!" Liam shrieked as he tried to stop Suzy entering the secret passage. But instead of stopping, she giggled, grabbed him and pulled him inside with her. He was still trying to wriggle out of her grasp when the bookcase slammed shut behind them. The two children were plunged into darkness.

"Oh well, that's just brilliant!" Liam snapped. "We'll be stuck in here forever now!"

He whirled round to touch the back of the bookcase. He was trying to feel for a button or for some machinery that would make the bookcase slide open again.

It was no good. The entrance to the secret passage was sealed!

Liam looked around in anguish. Then, suddenly, he was dazzled by a bright light. He quickly covered his eyes with his hands.

"Look!" said Suzy. "I found a torch."

Liam blinked. By the time he could see again, Suzy was waving the torch around. The ceiling of the passage in front of them was hung with thick, dusty cobwebs.

"Hey, do you think there are giant spiders in here?" she asked.

"Giant spiders?!" roared Liam. "We're in enough trouble as it is!"

"Calm down," said Suzy. "Isn't this like that thing in that book of yours? What did you call it? It's a bit like a treasure hunt but with …?"

"... but with all these dangers along the way," Liam said. "It's called a quest."

"A quest, that's right," said Suzy. She looked at Liam, puzzled. "I thought you liked adventures."

"I like *reading* about them!" Liam snapped. "I don't want to be actually in danger with no hope of being rescued."

Suzy thought about that for a moment and then she shrugged. "Suit yourself," she said, and she set off down the passage. "I'm going to find the Ghoul's Gold — providing the giant spiders don't get me first!"

Then she laughed. She actually laughed! Liam had never been so angry and scared, all at the same time. He tried to dissuade Suzy, but she wasn't listening. Liam didn't want to be left alone in the dark, so he ran after her.

As they went on, Liam noticed that the passage wasn't straight. It was curving and the walls weren't smooth. They were covered in bumps, like scales. It was as if they were walking inside the coils of a huge snake – or even a dragon!

Suddenly, Suzy stopped in her tracks. "Ah," she said. In front of her, the secret passage split into two. They had to choose which path to take.

Suzy had already thought of a way of choosing. She closed her eyes, turned on the spot and pointed.

"Wait!" said Liam. It was a scary experience being stuck in a dangerous place with someone who just kept making things worse. But at least it made you think! The door to the secret passage had opened when Suzy touched the copy of *Sir Kay and the Adventure of the Ghoul's Gold*. Perhaps there was a clue in that story. Liam racked his brains.

Then suddenly he saw it. A small silver dragon was caught in the torchlight, just where the passage divided. It was facing towards the right.

"Right, we go right!" said Liam. Before Suzy could argue with him, he grabbed her hand and pulled her with him.

"On his quest, Sir Kay has to find his way through the Dragon's Maze," Liam explained. "So if we follow the way the dragon is pointing …"

"… we might get eaten by dragons instead of giant spiders?" said Suzy. In the torchlight, Liam could see that she was smiling.

"Come on," said Liam solemnly. He didn't think this was a time for jokes.

The maze coiled and twisted. There were stairs to climb and dead ends to avoid. Each time they had to choose a path, a small silver dragon pointed the way. They walked for so long, however, that Liam began to think they'd taken the wrong path after all. Perhaps they'd be condemned to stay in the Dragon's Maze forever!

Then, at last, they turned a corner and saw a light at the end of the passage: the outline of a door. The two children ran towards it.

The next thing they knew, they were tumbling out into a large room.

Real secret rooms

This is Witley Park in Surrey in the UK. The owner, Whitaker Wright, was a very rich Victorian. He had a big garden with a lake, and he constructed a ballroom under the lake!

In Tudor times, people who disagreed with the king had to hide or they would be put in prison. This big house was owned by the Throckmorton family. They had a secret room constructed inside it for any of their friends who needed to hide.

Looking down into the secret room from above.

Chapter 4
The ghost

Liam wasn't sure where he was. The curtains in the room were drawn so he went over and pulled one back. Looking out of the window, he could see that they were up on the first floor.

Suzy, meanwhile, was rolling around on the floor giggling.

"What's the matter with you?" Liam asked.

"Well, didn't you think that was fun?" Suzy replied.

Fun?! Being terrified you'd never get out of a dark maze wasn't Liam's idea of fun!

It was strange, though. Liam had to admit he was tingling with an exhilarating new feeling. He'd been scared but he'd faced his fear and overcome it. Had Suzy been right, after all? Did Liam actually *like* adventures — not just in books, but real ones, with real dangers?

It was too much to think about now. "We need to find Mrs Rhodes," said Liam. "She'll be worried about us."

Suzy made a disappointed noise. "I want to finish our quest, and find the Ghoul's Gold," she said.

"There *is* no Ghoul's Gold," Liam snorted, going over to the door.

"There was a Dragon's Maze," said Suzy, "just like in your book. Maybe there'll be gold too — and a ghost guarding it!"

Liam shook his head. He reached for the door handle and tried to turn it — but the door was locked. "There might be some keys somewhere in this room," said Liam. "Let's have a look around."

The furniture was covered in large white sheets to protect it from dust. Liam and Suzy started pulling the sheets off. There might be some keys under one of them.

"Found anything?" Liam asked Suzy. When she didn't reply, he looked up at her. Suzy was pointing but it wasn't keys that she'd seen. Suzy's arm was shaking.

One of the dustsheets was rising up of its own accord and taking the shape of a …

"G-g-g-ghost!" Suzy stammered.

"There's no such thing as ghosts," said Liam.

"Tell that to the ghost!" said Suzy.

Slowly and silently, the ghost started to move towards her.

"We have to leave! How are we going to get out?!" Suzy cried, running over to Liam.

Liam didn't know what to do. The door was locked and they were too high up to jump out of the window.

"Think about the book," Suzy said. "Maybe there's a clue there. What happened after the Dragon's Maze?"

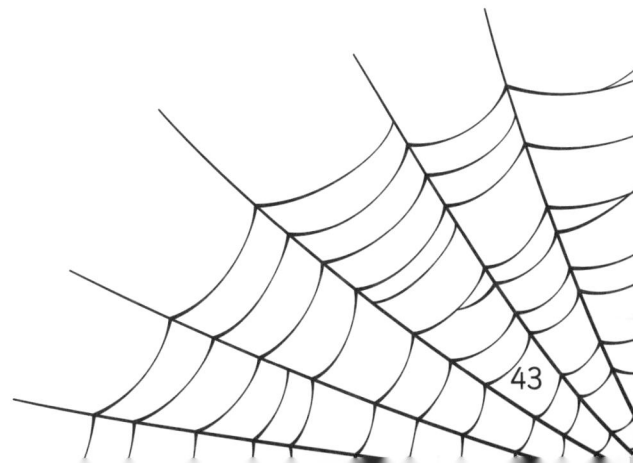

"The Spinning Fire!" said Liam. "After the Dragon's Maze, Sir Kay is faced with a solid wall of fire. He doesn't know how he's going to escape. Then it starts to spin, round and round, so that for just a few seconds, he can get past it — but only if he's quick."

"There isn't any fire in this room," said Suzy.

"No," said Liam, looking around, "but there is a fire*place*."

While he'd been thinking, the ghost had been getting closer. It was almost close enough to touch them now.

"Quick!" said Suzy.

Liam shrugged his backpack off, swung it round in the air and threw it at the ghost, who stumbled backwards.

That gave the two children just enough time. They ran past the ghost, and over to the fireplace on the other side of the room.

They skidded on the floor and crawled inside the fireplace. They got covered in soot and ash as they looked for some way to make it spin. The chimney above them was blocked so there was no way out there.

Liam looked up. The ghost was back on its feet and was making its way slowly, and surely, towards them.

"What if there *is* no Spinning Fire?" Liam wondered. "What if there's no escape?"

"There has to be," said Suzy. She was now beating at the metal plate at the back of the fireplace with her fists. Liam did the same.

The ghost was so close now.

Liam's hands were hurting. He needed something heavy to hit the metal plate with. He saw a basket of logs. He reached out and grabbed one.

That's when he realised – the log wasn't real, it was another lever. They heard the sound of antique machinery grinding into life and the fireplace started to spin – slowly at first, and then faster and faster.

"Hold on tight!" said Suzy.

The ghost groaned and rushed towards them.

Chapter 5
The horse

The fireplace was spinning very quickly now. Sometimes Liam and Suzy could see the room they were trying to escape *into*, sometimes they could see the room they were trying to escape *from*. The ghost had lurched backwards as the fireplace picked up speed, but it was still waiting for them. Both rooms were flashing by, faster and faster.

"I don't know when to jump!" shouted Liam.

"That's your problem," said Suzy, "you think too much!"

She grabbed his hand and they jumped.

They landed, gasping and spluttering from the soot and ash, but they had obviously ended up in the right room. It was full of old toys, games and books. There was even a rocking horse. This must have been the nursery, where Guy Languish's children would have played in Victorian times.

Liam looked back. The fireplace was spinning slower and slower now. Beyond it, in the locked room, the ghost was bending down. It was trying to get through the fireplace to reach them. As Liam watched, the fireplace shuddered precariously. At last, it came to a stop, sealing up the room.

"Let's hope it's not the kind of ghost that can walk through walls," said Suzy.

"Is that a helpful thing to say?" asked Liam.

"Sorry," said Suzy.

"It's all right," said Liam.

"No, I mean it," said Suzy. "I thought books were boring, and they're not. We're having an amazing adventure because of them."

"I thought you were always getting into trouble," said Liam, "and you're not — you're brave."

"I can get into trouble as well," said Suzy, with a smile.

"Friends?" asked Liam. Suzy nodded and they shook hands.

"So, do you believe me now about the existence of the Ghoul's Gold?" asked Suzy.

"I think we should get back to Mrs Rhodes," said Liam. "Let's just hope this door is unlocked."

"Oh, it's unlocked all right," said Suzy. She pointed to where the door was creaking open. The ghost began to glide into the room.

"Give us a break!" said Liam.

"Looks like we're going to have to continue our quest after all," said Suzy.

Liam was trying to remember what Sir Kay had to face next in the story. "Pegasus!" he said. "Sir Kay had to fly on Pegasus!"

"Brilliant!" said Suzy. "Who's Peggy's sis?"

"Seriously? We did this last week!" said Liam. "Our topic this term is the Greek myths."

"Yes, but I wasn't paying attention, was I?" said Suzy, as if he'd just said the silliest thing.

"Pegasus was a flying horse," said Liam.

The ghost was between them and the door. There had to be another way out, but where?

"Found it!" Suzy sang out. She was sitting on the rocking horse.

"*Flying* horse," said Liam, "not *rocking* horse!" There was scarcely enough room for the two of them on its back!

Suzy pointed at the ghost and shouted, "No time to argue!"

Liam jumped on behind her. A chain hung loosely from the ceiling, attached to the back of the rocking horse. Suddenly, it went taut and started to pull the horse upwards.

"Yay!" cried Suzy.

Liam looked up. They were heading for the ceiling very fast!

Liam and Suzy covered their heads with their arms. Just as they were about to hit the ceiling, however, a small flap opened directly above them. The chain yanked the rocking horse up through the opening so sharply that the children slipped off its back. They hung for a moment, clinging on to the horse's feet. It was a long drop back down to the nursery – and the waiting ghost.

Just in time, though, the flap slapped shut beneath them.

They looked around. They were in the attic. Little windows in the slanted roof let some light in so they weren't lost in the dark, but it didn't look very promising. There were boxes everywhere, broken furniture, paintings covered in cobwebs and dust; it was a collection of forgotten and unneeded things.

"He couldn't have hidden the Ghoul's Gold here, could he?" wondered Suzy. "What's the next clue?"

"I don't know, do I?" Liam replied. "Sir Kay had one last challenge to face, but you were being so annoying on the coach that I didn't finish the story."

"Oh," said Suzy. "Sorry."

Real lost treasure

The Ghoul's Gold isn't the only treasure to have been lost. Throughout history, valuable objects were stolen, or hidden, and forgotten about. Here are some …

King John's crown jewels

In 1216, King John of England was retreating from his enemies. It's said that he was trying to cross a stretch of water called the Wash when the tide rose and the wagon carrying his crown jewels was lost.

The wreck of *San Miguel*

A ship called *San Miguel* was sailing from Cuba to Spain in 1551. It was caught in a hurricane and sank. In today's money, its lost cargo of gold and silver would be worth billions.

The sceptre of Dagobert

This golden sceptre was part of the French crown jewels for over a thousand years! It was stolen in 1795 and was never seen again …

Chapter 6
The treasure

Liam still wasn't convinced that there was any truth in the legend of the Ghoul's Gold. Would a distinguished Victorian writer really hide treasure somewhere in his house and leave clues in one of his books? Maybe. After all, Liam wasn't persuaded about ghosts either, and that hadn't stopped a ghost chasing him around all morning!

"I've just thought!" said Suzy. "If you were reading the book on the coach, you must still have it. We can look up the last clue."

"The book is in my backpack – " Liam began.

"Great!" said Suzy.

"That I threw at the ghost downstairs," Liam finished.

Still, Suzy wouldn't give up. She started walking around the attic, looking for a clue.

"What was the last thing you remember reading?" she asked.

"I couldn't concentrate enough to read," Liam replied. "I was just staring at one of the pictures."

"This Kay is a knight, right?" Suzy asked.

"Yes," said Liam. "He's *Sir* Kay. Why?"

Suzy was crouched in front of one of
the paintings, wiping cobwebs off it with her sleeve.
"Does he look like this?"

Liam peered at the picture curiously. It was
the one he'd been looking at in the book! Sir Kay was
standing in front of the final challenge of the story.

"A waterfall!" said Suzy and Liam together. They rushed out of the attic and down through the house, heading towards the gardens.

As they sprinted towards the main door, they passed Mrs Rhodes and the rest of the children.

"What happened to you two?" Mrs Rhodes asked. "You're filthy!" She was going to give them a telling off, but the ghost burst out of a door in front of her. Mrs Rhodes shrieked and started hitting it with her clipboard.

Liam and Suzy ran out into the garden. They were panting when they reached the waterfall.

"What do we do now?" Suzy shouted over the din. "We'll get soaked! Crushed even!"

"We are knights of honour," Liam shouted back. "We'll be brave and complete our quest."

They breathed deeply and walked towards the waterfall. Just as they were about to go through it, Liam stepped on something that pivoted like a pedal, and the waterfall stopped.

Behind it, hidden since Victorian times, was a cave. Liam and Suzy went in.

Suddenly, a towering silhouette loomed out of the shadows. It was dressed head to toe in black.

"Sir Grotesque Ghoul, the Ghost Knight!" gasped Liam.

The children stepped backwards in fright.
Then they heard a creaking, tearing sound.
The knight's breastplate split open, revealing rusting machinery inside. Behind him, they could see a large box full of gold coins.

"I told you there was treasure!" said Suzy.

"He's been guarding it all these years," said Liam.

"And now it's mine," said a voice behind them.

They whirled round to see the silhouette of the ghost.

"I've been looking for that treasure for years," it said. "Why else do you think I took a job in a boring writer's boring old house?"

"I didn't know being a ghost was a job," said Liam.

"Oh, Liam," said Suzy. "It's a disguise! How many ghosts wear trainers?"

Liam looked at the ghost's feet. "Mary?!" he said.

"I dress up as the ghost to enhance the visitors' experience," said Mary. "But when I heard you two talking about clues to finding the treasure, I thought you might be on to something, so I followed you."

"You should have read a few of the boring old writer's boring old books," said Suzy. "All the clues were there. You'd be a rich woman now."

"I *am* a rich woman," Mary insisted. "Who's going to stop me taking the treasure — a pair of little kids like you?"

Mary pushed past them, but the floor of the cave was wet from the waterfall. Her trainers slipped and she staggered backwards. She must have stepped on the pedal because the waterfall started again, and crashed down on top of her. Mary was flushed out into the garden, where Mrs Rhodes and the other children found her, spluttering and furious.

After she'd spoken to the police, Mrs Rhodes told Suzy and Liam that they'd get a reward for finding the treasure.

"What will you spend it on?" asked Liam.

"Books," said Suzy. "What about you?"

"Adventures," said Liam, "but only if you'll share them with me."

The secrets of Gothic Grange

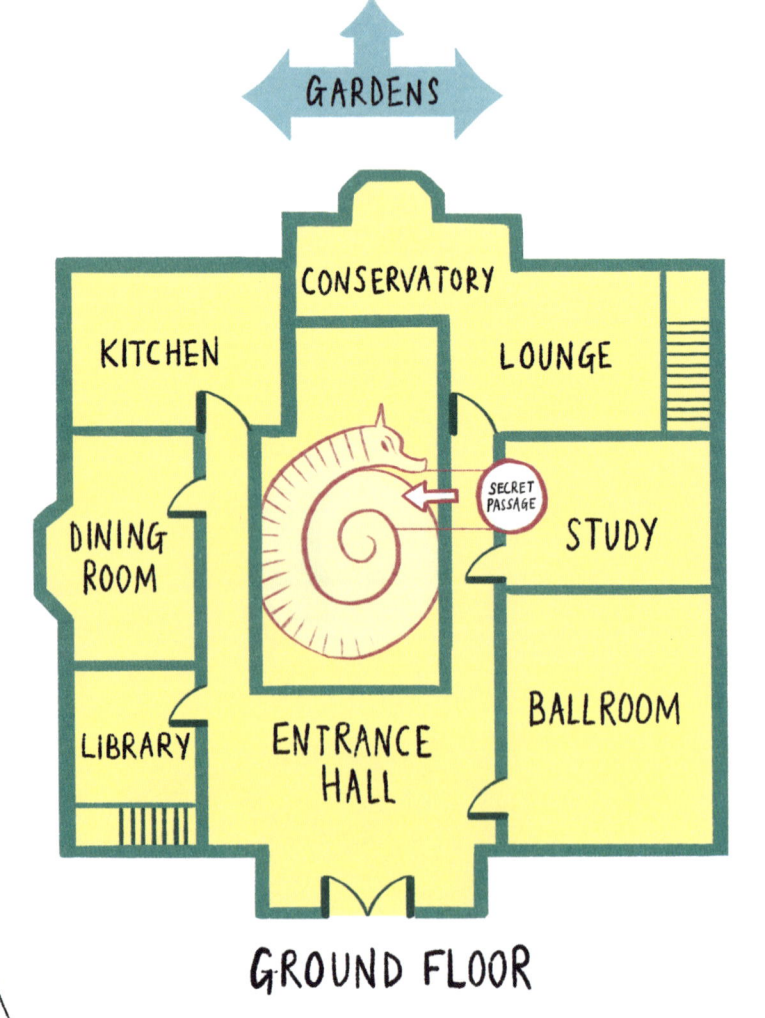

GARDENS

CONSERVATORY

KITCHEN

LOUNGE

SECRET PASSAGE

DINING ROOM

STUDY

LIBRARY

ENTRANCE HALL

BALLROOM

GROUND FLOOR

GARDENS

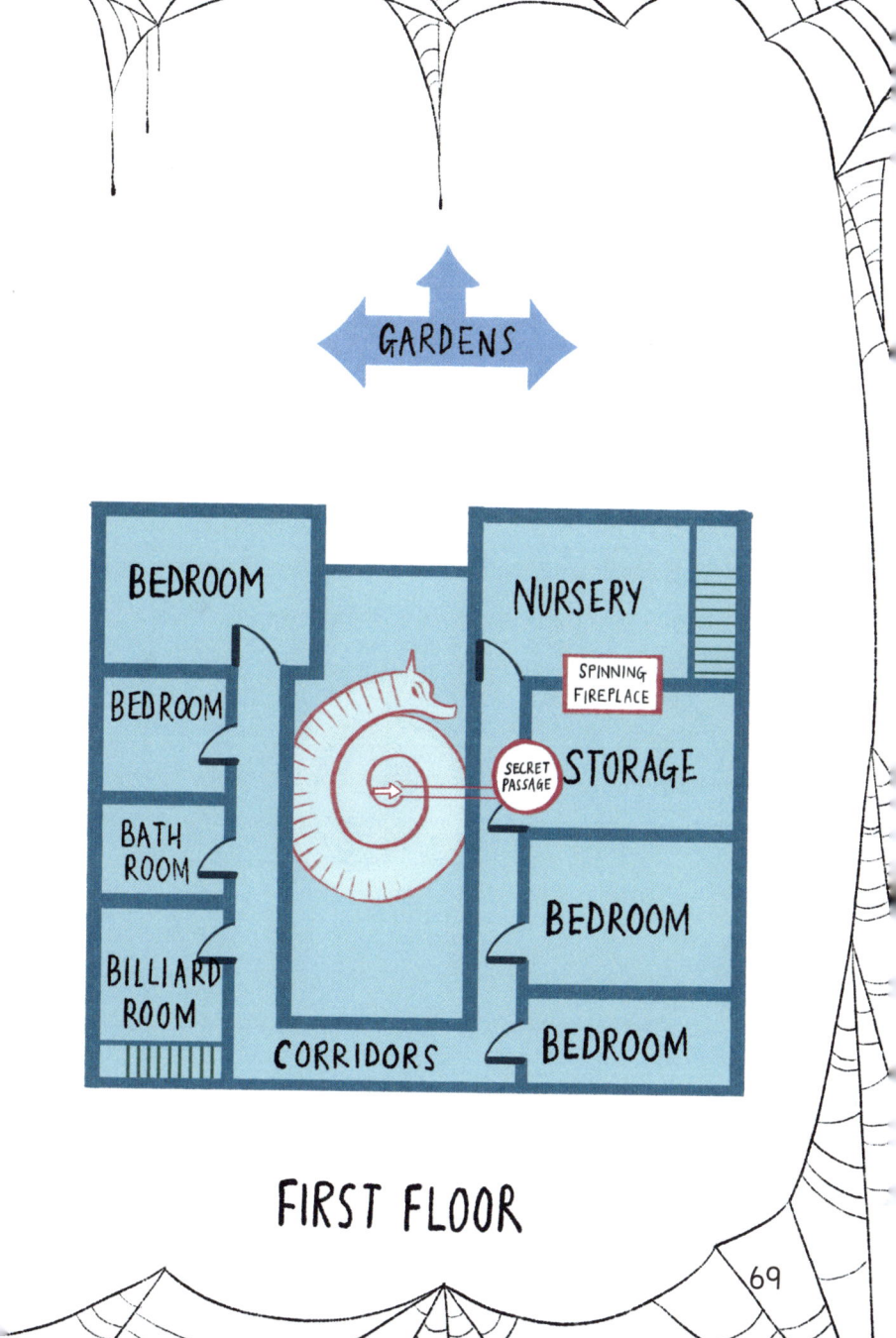

BEDROOM

BEDROOM

BATH ROOM

BILLIARD ROOM

NURSERY

SPINNING FIREPLACE

SECRET PASSAGE

STORAGE

BEDROOM

BEDROOM

CORRIDORS

FIRST FLOOR

About the author

What do you like best about writing?

Writing is a great way to do lots of exciting things without ever leaving the safety of your room. I'm like Liam in the story: I'm an armchair adventurer. I'm too cowardly to go on an actual adventure – they're dangerous! – but if I write a story, I can go anywhere and do anything. That's the wonderful thing about writing. It's total freedom. If you can think it, it happens.

Timothy Knapman

How did you come up with the idea for this story?

I was thinking about armchair adventurers, like me and Liam, and how we're not like people who have *actual* adventures. I've met a few real adventurers in my time. I once met a man who paddled down the Amazon and slept with crocodiles. Liam isn't that sort of person at all. He's careful, he thinks a lot and he's easily scared because he knows that things can go wrong. On the other hand, Suzy does things without thinking, and sometimes that can lead to an adventure. As the story went along, I wanted the two of them, Suzy and Liam, to appreciate what is good about one another. It's good to think, to be careful, but it's also good to be brave and to take a chance now and then.

Have you ever been to a big old house like Gothic Grange?

I love big old houses – especially ones with stories attached to them, where famous and interesting people have lived. I don't know a single house that has as many secrets and surprises as Gothic Grange. I made it up out of bits of different houses.

Have you ever seen a secret room or passage?

A few – and they tend to be a bit small and dirty. People don't bother decorating them because they're places you only go when you're hiding from danger, or when you don't want people to see you. There's one secret passage that I really want to visit but whenever I've tried it's been closed. It's in the city of Florence, in Italy, and it's called the Vasari Corridor. It leads from the town hall – where all the important decisions were taken – to the palace of the family that ruled Florence for many years. They liked art and so the Vasari Corridor is beautifully decorated.

What do you hope readers will get out of the book?

I hope they'll appreciate people who are different from them and understand that being different can be a good thing. People who are not like us can help us do things we can't usually do. They can make us brighter, better, braver people.

About the illustrator

What made you want to be an illustrator?

As a child, I had a set of classic fairytale books with beautiful illustrations that really sparked my imagination. I loved looking at colours, so drawing with felt tips and crayons was something I did every day. The more I drew, the more I realised I wanted to do it professionally.

Maxine Lee-Mackie

What did you like best about illustrating this book?

I really enjoyed illustrating the dusty attic scenes. Especially the one where Suzy spots Sir. Arthur Kay giving them a clue!

What was the most difficult thing about illustrating this book?

When a story is set inside a house, it's important to make sure the rooms, corridors and secret passages are all in the right place. I had to make lots of sketches and plans to make sure I get this right.

How do you bring a character to life in an illustration?

I think about what the characters would sound like, how they would move, and their facial expressions. Sometimes I make the faces myself as a I draw (I hope no-one can see me!).

Have you ever been to a big old house like Gothic Grange?

I have – there is a place called Speke Hall near where I live. It's a huge house with beautiful gardens, woodland and a maze and it even has a secret passage!

Are you an armchair adventurer, like Liam, or do you prefer real adventure, like Suzy?

I think I'm a little bit like both of them. I do love to read and get lost in other people's stories, but I also like to be on adventures of my own when I can.

Which of the scenes was the most fun to draw, and why?

I like the darker scenes the best. I love to draw cobwebs, shadows, and light, so the secret passages and attic space were a lot of fun. I really enjoyed experimenting with ways to make the torchlight glow.

Book chat

Have you ever been to an old house like Gothic Grange? What was it like?

What skills did Liam and Suzy each bring to the adventure?

Do you think any of the characters changed from the start of the book to the end?

If you could ask the author or illustrator a question, what would you ask?

Does this book remind you of any other stories you know? How?

How did you feel at different points of the story?

If you could talk to one character from the book, who would you choose? What would you ask?

What did you think of the book at the start? Did you change your mind as you read it?

Book challenge:

Draw a floor plan for your own old house, complete with secret passages and rooms.

Published by Collins
An imprint of HarperCollins*Publishers*

The News Building
1 London Bridge Street
London SE1 9GF
UK

Macken House
39/40 Mayor Street Upper
Dublin 1
D01 C9W8
Ireland

Text © Timothy Knapman 2024
Design and illustrations © HarperCollins*Publishers* Limited 2024

10 9 8 7 6 5 4 3 2 1

ISBN 978-0-00-868123-4

All rights reserved. No part of this publication may be reproduced, stored in a retrieval system, or transmitted in any form by any means, electronic, mechanical, photocopying, recording or otherwise, without the prior written permission of the Publisher or a licence permitting restricted copying in the United Kingdom issued by the Copyright Licensing Agency Ltd, 5th Floor, Shackleton House, 4 Battle Bridge Lane, London SE1 2HX.

British Library Cataloguing-in-Publication Data
A catalogue record for this publication is available from the British Library.

Download the teaching notes and word cards to accompany this book at:
http://littlewandle.org.uk/signupfluency/

Get the latest Collins Big Cat news at
collins.co.uk/collinsbigcat

Author: Timothy Knapman
Illustrator: Maxine Lee-Mackie
Publisher: Laura White
Product manager and
 commissioning editor: Caroline Green
Series editor: Charlotte Raby
Development editor: Catherine Baker
Project manager: Emily Hooton
Copyeditor: Sally Byford
Proofreader: Catherine Dakin
Cover designer: Sarah Finan
Typesetter: 2Hoots Publishing Services Ltd
Production controller: Katharine Willard

Printed in the UK.

MIX
Paper | Supporting responsible forestry
FSC™ C007454

This book is produced from independently certified FSC™ paper to ensure responsible forest management.

For more information visit: www.harpercollins.co.uk/green

Made with responsibly sourced paper and vegetable ink

Scan to see how we are reducing our environmental impact.

Acknowledgements
The publishers gratefully acknowledge the permission granted to reproduce the copyright material in this book. Every effort has been made to trace copyright holders and to obtain their permission for the use of copyright material. The publishers will gladly receive any information enabling them to rectify any error or omission at the first opportunity.

p26l SCStock/Shutterstock, p26r Akane1988/Shutterstock, p27t Hemis/Alamy, p27b Frederic Legrand-COMEO/Shutterstock, p36t ANL/Shutterstock, p36b ANL/Shutterstock, p37t The National Trust Photolibrary/Alamy, p37b David Hughes/Shutterstock, p56 Timewatch Images/Alamy, p57l De Luan/Alamy, p57r Florilegius/Alamy.